Fifteen-Minute Fiction: a flash fiction anthology

CW01501201

WHAT THE

Aira is a performance marketing agency nestled among the herds of concrete cows in the centre of Milton Keynes, UK. One service we offer our wonderful clients is copywriting, which is something that we think we're fairly good at.

Every Friday the Aira copywriting team partakes in something we call *Flash Fiction Friday* and spends just 15 minutes writing a piece of flash fiction, with each writer working to the same prompt.

It could be anything, from space toilets to memorable car rides – anything can inspire us. It helps keep our writing sharp and our creative muscles constantly flexed, enabling us to always deliver the best work for our clients. Also, it reminds us that copywriting can be fun and creative, which in turn helps with engagement.

This book is a collection of some of our favourite #flashfictionfriday pieces.

For more information visit www.aira.net

Fifteen-Minute Fiction: a flash fiction anthology

Fifteen-Minute Fiction
a flash fiction anthology

Sam JT Butterworth

Lucy Hancock

Mike Jeavons

Hannah Hopkins Jones

Fifteen-Minute Fiction: a flash fiction anthology

CONTENTS

Fifteen-Minute Fiction: a flash fiction anthology

FOREWORD
BY PADDY MOOGAN
AIRA'S CEO AND CO-FOUNDER

Few would argue about the importance of creativity in marketing. Standing out from the crowd, particularly online where we're constantly bombarded with notifications, information and marketing messages, is more important than ever and has been since I can remember.

The thing is, as someone whose roots stem from technical SEO and the early days of paid media, I don't think I ever appreciated the importance of copywriting in the bigger picture of marketing. I saw copy as rather functional and to serve a specific purpose: to get people to do the thing I wanted them to do (usually buy my client's product!).

Maybe it was due to my inexperience, topped up with the industry's tendency to focus on shiny technology and software, that led to this underappreciation of copywriting. Now, it's almost embarrassing to admit that I held this view because I've seen first-hand what the power of great copywriting can do to a business. In fact, the team at Aira do this and I see the results that they drive for our clients every single day.

Great copywriting can help a business connect with their target audience at every stage of the journey they take in buying a product or service. Whether it's that very first moment where someone realises that they have a problem that they want to solve, or as they're about to get out their credit card to buy a product, copy plays an important role.

Get it wrong, and you'll lose the customer, possibly forever. Get it right, and you may well have a customer for life.

But getting it right isn't easy and keeping your copywriting skills fresh and relevant takes a lot of effort. Creativity can often feel like something that does (or doesn't) come naturally but in reality, it's useful to think about it as a muscle that you can exercise and keep in good shape, as opposed to something that just happens.

One way that our copywriting team at Aira does this is to take 15 minutes each week to write about a random topic in a creative way. What follows is a collection of the results of those sessions which, as you'll see, enable the team to challenge themselves each and every week with topics that range from weird to wonderful and to exercise their creative muscles, ultimately leading to more creativity in their work for our clients.

prompt one

space toilet

Fifteen-Minute Fiction: a flash fiction anthology

NO WARRANTY
by Hannah Hopkins Jones

Congratulations!

You are now the owner of the brand new, limited edition **DYNAMIC DISCO DEFECATOR 3000**. Enclosed you will find a user manual, which includes a QR code that will grant you access to the online training materials you will need to operate your new toilet.

Online training materials include:

- 30+ hours of instructional videos.
- 3 multiple choice question exams.
- A downloadable certificate for you to keep on completion of your training.

After you have earned your **DYNAMIC DISCO DEFECATOR 3000** operator certification, you will be able to use your new toilet not just for 1s and 2s, but as a **gateway to multiple dimensions**. Customisable settings allow you to chart the direction of your interdimensional journey, choose the music you wish to play on departure and arrival, and design the unique signal you wish to broadcast across multiple universes to announce your exploration.

CAUTION

If you choose to broadcast your signal across the universes, there is a chance that it will gain the attention of other interdimensional travellers. We cannot guarantee that other travellers will comply with the **DYNAMIC DISCO DEFECATOR 3000** code of conduct, and are not liable for any negative interactions, or butterfly-effect equivalent consequences that may occur on your travels.

To return home at any time, simply wipe and flush, and remember to wash your hands once you have returned to your bathroom. If you see your reflection in your bathroom mirror and experience a growing sense of dread, please contact our helpline.

*Possible side effects of piloting the **DYNAMIC DISCO DEFECATOR 3000** may include but are not limited to: pain; anguish; existential dread; feeling the heavy weight of the world upon your shoulders; insomnia; eczema; discolouration of your hair and nails; alienation from friends and family; inability to differentiate between what is real and what is not; shortness of breath; numbness in the extremities; enhanced vision; enhanced visions; the appearance of dark figures lurking in your peripheral vision; bad breath; and nausea.*

TALKING TOILET
by Lucy Hancock

Polly had always struggled to make friends. Not that she minded - she never experienced loneliness as such. But this meant she'd grown accustomed to spending each lunch break in a different area of the school.

Monday, she hid in the library. This was one of her favourite lunch spots. The librarian was always friendly (except for when Polly got crumbs on the carpet) and it was definitely one of the more hygienic makeshift cafeteria options. What wasn't, you guessed it, was the toilet cubicle. This, she saved for Wednesdays. After all, you couldn't spend every lunch time in the same spot - you'd start to look... like you didn't have any friends.

Wednesday came around and Polly made her way to the fifth toilet cubicle in the West block. She chose this particular cubicle because it always had an 'out of order' sign displayed proudly on the door, so no one would knock or try and disturb her moment of peace and crisps munching. As you can probably expect, Polly got through a lot of hand sanitiser. As she put the toilet seat down to get comfortable, she squeezed a large dollop of crisp apple hand gel on her palms. Next, she unwrapped her tuna sandwich and began to munch as quietly as possible.

That was, until she heard a voice that made her nearly fall off the loo.

"Hi."

Polly's eyes scanned the cubicle in panic, as if someone had the space to hide in there with her.

Polly inhaled deeply, trying to calm her racing heart. She took another bite of her sandwich before she unzipped her rucksack, preparing for an escape.

"Yes, you," the voice continued. "You're here every week, aren't you?"

Polly gulped. Her voice, quiet and mouse-like, just about escaped her mouth. "Yes," she whispered. Her eyes continued to scan the cubicle.

Polly thought this must be a really strange dream, because the voice sounded like it was coming from… the toilet.

THE ADVENTURES OF SPACE TOILET
by Mike Jeavons

When I sat down on the toilet I expected to experience the brief euphoria that usually happened upon myself around an hour or two after I'd finished the first coffee of the day. That is, I was looking forward to a good shit.

However, this morning things were a little different.

I missed the bus, so I was gonna be late for work. Worse still, I'd already downed my double macchiato with oat milk and an extra shot of espresso, and I knew that not only would this delay put me in hot water with my boss, but it would also put me in hot water with my underwear.

So, I had to do the unimaginable. I'd have to rely on the bus station toilets, which were perpetually cold and had burned the sweet smell of ammonia into my nostrils before I'd even opened the door.

A man smiled at me. I wondered if he was waiting for someone to get into the far stall, which I knew for a fact had a glory hole in it. There was no time for fun; it was time for business.

There was no seat, so I had to rest my peachy cheeks on the icy porcelain. I grimaced, but I had little choice. The train had already left the station (which is ironic considering I was in a bus station).

But then, as my fecal matter kissed the yellow water at the base

7

of the bowl, the graffiti-laden walls of the stall changed. Gone were the felt tip penises and mobile phone numbers offering me a good time.

Instead, I was in deep space.

And it was beautiful. Distant stars twinkled like disco balls partying in passing galaxies. Planets hung in nothingness hiding secrets yet to be discovered. A meteor shot by leaving a trail as bright as the future I thought I had before me until I missed that bloody bus.

I tensed my bum and the poo sploshed into the water.

Then, I was back. The majesty of outer space was gone.

Instead, I was in freezing cold public toilets of my local bus station.

What the hell just happened? How had it happened? And why?

There was a knock on the stall door. Was I about to get my answer?

"Wanna use the glory hole?" they asked.

"Not today," I replied.

PLEASE WELCOME, SPACE TOILET
by Sam JT Butterworth

Groucho's had sticky floors and sweaty ceilings when the place was full, which it was tonight. There was a palpable excitement and apprehension too, as people chatted loudly over the last song of the support band, Dog's Dinner. Ten minutes later people were returning from the bar with armfuls of overpriced, watered-down lager and trying to find their friends for the main event.

'Ladies and gentlemen,' came the disembodied announcement. 'Hope you're ready to get weird! Please welcome, Space Toilet!'

The unified crowd roared and whooped and smiled widely as Space Toilet bounced onto the stage, grinning a wide, confident smile.

'Alright you fuckers - have some of this!'

There followed a sound so raw, affecting and beautiful that while the crowd danced to the uptempo beat, most were simultaneously brought to tears. Newbies who hadn't seen Space Toilet before were wide-eyed, not believing what they saw, while veteran fans were blown away by the consistent brilliance of this unique act.

After an hour the fans were wading in an inch of water, beer, tears and fresh urine, and it was getting deeper all the time. After two hours it was up to their knees, but on they danced, as much liquid coming from the stage, where Space Toilet sprayed the crowd endlessly from its glittering, overflowing basin. Where did it all come from? It wasn't even plumbed in!

After three hours the set was over and the audience stood in awe, wading up to their waists, but still happy and excited for the final part of the act they all knew was coming.

'Flush, flush, flush!' they called as one. And after a moment Space Toilet grabbed his chrome flush and yanked. Immediately a maelstrom opened up in the crowd and one by one, each ecstatic member of the audience was drawn down into another world of joy, peace and animated multidimensional toilets.

prompt two
the floor smells like

Fifteen-Minute Fiction: a flash fiction anthology

BUSTED
by Mike Jeavons

'Who the hell broke the lamp?'

Mum's right eye twitched the way it only did when she was really angry, like the time my brother Johnny accidentally set fire to the carpet in the spare room. And when he pulled the radiator off the wall on the landing. And when he kicked our cat, Jeff, down the stairs. And now.

'Not me,' I said, knowing full well it was Johnny who had broken the lamp, on account of the fact that I'd just watched him do it.

Mum looked at Johnny, who sat cross-legged on the sofa, humming to himself as he kept his eyes on the TV and shovelled cheesy Wotsits into his mouth from a bowl.

'Johnny?' asked Mum with a *tone*.

I popped a salt and vinegar crisp into my mouth and watched the emerging argument.

'Yes?'

'Did you break the lamp?'

'What lamp?' he asked.

He was overdoing it. She was never going to believe him.

Mum nodded to the lamp, her eye twitch getting twitchier.

'No,' said Johnny, his mouth dropping open like it was the first time he'd even seen a lamp.

'Are you sure?' asked Mum.

Johnny nodded.

I smirked.

Mum bent down and fished a bouncy ball from beneath the side table where the lamp was. She picked it up and her mouth twisted in a *gotcha* kind of way.

Johnny shrugged.

Mum sighed and sniffed the ball. Then she bent down again and smelled the spot on the floor around the shards of the broken vase.

'Huh,' muttered Mum. She looked at me. 'Simon, why do this bouncy ball and the floor smell like salt and vinegar?'

Oh shit, I thought.

THE FLOOR SMELLS LIKE A CAT HAS BEEN SICK THROUGH A LEMON
by Sam JT Butterworth

'The floor smells like a cat has been sick through a lemon,' he said. 'I don't see what's wrong with normal bleach. How's this improving our olfactory experience?'

'Christ Jim,' Mona said. 'Buy your own bleach if you like. Even better, clean up the cat sick yourself. It was your idea to get the little shit.'

Mona half-threw, half-skidded the mop across the slick grey, vinyl floor and it clattered against the side of the plate cupboard. Then she walked out of the room in her old open-toed slippers, the white fur now a mottled beige - not unlike Banjo, the culprit cat.

Jim stood there, his coat still on, regretting his words. He wondered why he couldn't resist his outbursts, when all he really wanted to do was kiss his girlfriend and plan something fun they could do for the rest of the evening. Now he'd have to apologise and try and start the night off again.

Christ, the room still stinks, he thought, glad Mona wasn't in the room in case he said it out loud, which he probably would.

He took two beers from the fridge and went through to the living room. Banjo was sitting on Mona's knee as if he was completely innocent and Jim felt like throwing one of the bottles at him. Instead he closed his eyes and breathed. Then he opened them and smiled at Mona, giving her the beer. He sat down next to her and stroked the cat, which hissed and slashed his hand, then departed.

EMO CONCERT
by Lucy Hancock

Teenagers instinctively craving freedom, in need of just a few hours away from the confinement of homework and Mum's weekly roast. A field of clear skies or empty beach isn't enough escapism to mend their heartbreak from the boy in Maths that dumped them over text.

Instead, there is no better way to feel whole than to be crammed like a bee-hive in a room with strobe lights and a singer that sounds like Rod Stewart has been mixed with black treacle and Halloween.

All of our Christmas money going on one ticket, a way out from people who don't *get* us and friends who forgot our birthday. Our bodies are the closest they've been to someone in months, for Mum's hugs are something we avoid as she's *so embarrassing*.

The air smells like sweat and a man who clearly owns *several* cats. The girl next to you has eyes that have been circled with at least two pots of eyeliner and a mouth that doesn't smile because smiling isn't cool.

… and the floor smells like Heineken and looks like piss.

prompt three
write one sentence, carry it on 1

Fifteen-Minute Fiction: a flash fiction anthology

HAVE YOU SEEN MY BUGLE?

by Sam JT Butterworth, Lucy Hancock, Mike Jeavons and Hannah
Hopkins Jones, each taking turns to write one sentence

A loud cry echoed in the mist. **A cry I'd heard before.** *I could*
understand why it was often called a 'bugle', though rarely had I heard it be so
melodic. To my untrained ears, I could swear there were notes to
'Dancing Queen' by Abba in there. Something rustled in the bushes.
Then the sound came again, closer. *I was grateful that I hadn't*
ventured so far out on my own.

'Have you seen my bugle?' asked John, emerging from the tent.

'Can't say I have, no.' I replied, staring at my phone screen.

'Well you're not gonna bloody find it there are you!?'

I shrugged, glancing towards the bushes where I had first heard the rustling.
Suddenly, the rustling became a bang, and I leaped back in shock.

'It's not bonfire night, is it?' asked John, my younger, less-
attractive brother.

'Not tonight, ugly,' I said, peering back out into the night,
now just beyond the bushes.

We were on a tight schedule, but you wouldn't have been able to tell by John's
behaviour. For some reason he insisted on playing on his Gameboy
when we should have been investigating the banging bush. You'd

think he was six years old, but he's actually turning thirty two tomorrow.

'Right,' I said. 'I'm off to find out what the flipping heck is going on out there, with or without you.'

'If there really had been the option of doing this without me, I'd have stayed at home,' sighed John.

I rolled my eyes and edged towards the bush. If you were **wondering what the purpose of this camping trip was, we're looking for UFOs.**

'OK, you grab the tin foil hats John, I'll bring the chainsaw.'

John pulled his crumpled hat from his pocket, adjusting the coat hanger antenna. I needed to hurry the story along, so I approached the bush, grabbed the nearest branch, and yanked it to one side. And there it was, the source of the racket.

A tiny, yet now unbelievably loud UFO resembling a silver Babybel (as in the cheese). *Where the waxen seal would break a mouth appeared, and screamed.*

The words will stick with me forever.

'Get off my planet, you oaf!'

22

prompt four
fantasy endeavours

BLORKO'S TREATMENT
by Mike Jeavons

Blorko was a troll who had two very smelly feet.
All the other woodland creatures never could compete.

'Blorko why do your feet always smell so bloomin' bad?'
asked Blorko's friend who told him that his feet made him feel sad.

But Blorko didn't want his feet to smell for miles and miles,
He didn't want frowns when he neared, he wanted smiles and smiles.

So Blorko went to Aqua Fern, the only woodland spa,
Where he rested by the pool and soaked himself in tar.

Then it came to Blorko's feet, where Zing the bat stood by,
Zing was worried there was no hope, but would definitely try.

He scrubbed and scrubbed until his hands were tired and red and sore,
But holy heck, if they weren't less smelly than they were before.

Blorko left the spa so happy, it was such a massive win.
But not for Zing who bent over and threw up right in the bin.

Fifteen-Minute Fiction: a flash fiction anthology

ENOKI TALES
by Sam JT Butterworth

The mushroom smiled at me. He then smiled at two small mushrooms in the grass, before ripping them root-and-all out of the earth and devouring them. They squeaked as they went into his wide, black mouth, whose white teeth were small and sharp and multitudinous. He burped loudly, picked up his book, which he'd left face down on the turf, then went back to smiling.

What the fuck's going on?

I squinted my hazy eyes at the cover of the book. I could make out an M and then lots of small letters. I leaned closer and the mushroom spoke at the exact time I recognised the shapes of the words. Both said, 'Mind your own fucking business!'

Jesus Christ. I looked around at the forest of silver birches that encircled me and blocked out the sun and panic started to set in (more deeply). What was I doing again? How did I get here? I thought I was with...

'What's the book about?' I said.

The mushroom glanced at me over the page he was on, closed it on his thumb to hold his place and frowned at me.

'It's all about you and the awful thing that happens to you,' he said.

'What do you mean?!'

'Oh nothing, just the thing that's going to happen to you.'

'What? When?!'

'Have you got a watch?'

'I looked where my wrist usually was but instead I only found a pulsating white mushroom stalk. I grabbed at it and rubbed it and felt the soft, fibrous skin begin to disintegrate. I pulled my fingers away but they weren't fingers. They were slender, slithering enoki mushrooms that moved independent of my thought.

The mushroom had picked his book back up and was reading again.

'What happens next?' I said.

'Oh,' he laughed. 'This is a good bit, look down there.'

I looked down at a patch of leaf-strewn grass but as I did it receded as I grew upwards through the canopy of the trees, which weren't silver birches at all, but manure-speckled mushrooms. From up there the forest looked like an enormous cloud, and I let myself fall into it and float away.

THE HOUSE WITH LEGS
by Lucy Hancock

It was a thing of legend. The stuff of nightmares. The subject of songs. Every family, in every district of Earlsgarden spoke of it. It was the bedtime story told every year, on that fateful night of October 31st. Once the candles sat in pumpkins were blown out and the clock struck nine, children hid under their duvets and awaited the same tale they'd heard many times before.

'Mummy, do we really need to hear it *again*?' The girl sighed, for these types of stories just weren't cool enough anymore.

'Why of course,' her Mother smiled, squeezing her tightly. 'It's tradition.'

'But can it have a new ending or something?' The girl's brother replied, slurping his hot chocolate.

Her Mother shook her head. 'It ends exactly how it is meant to.'

There was a house that stood on a hill, in a hidden forest. Its large chimney blew thick, black fog across the trees and its door was always left ajar. Through the cracks in the door, you could make out a dim glow.

'What about the legs, Mummy? Tell us about the legs!' The girl giggled, tugging at the duvet.

The house on the hill was guarded by a large, bellowing tiger. And what was the tiger's favourite thing to eat?

'Children!' both children screamed in delight.

ADRIFT
by Hannah Hopkins Jones

At first it felt as though their prayers had been answered. The old tug had been adrift for several days, its engines irreparably damaged by a sudden squall, when they first felt the pull on the anchor.

Several members of the small and tired crew insisted it was a trick at first - there are so many ways that time spent at sea can play tricks on you - but when the water began to whiten at the prow and the air began to sting their faces even they couldn't deny it. The boat was being towed. The dark shadow beneath the surface remained there no matter how the sun moved, and the occasional slap of a tail's spiked sail just off of the stern confirmed their superstitions.

People celebrated. Songs were sung, wine was poured - an old god had come from the depths to steer them to safety. It happened in the stories. If it wanted to sink them and swallow them whole, surely it would have done so already?

The first sighting of land brought further jubilation, spurred on by the creeping delirium that comes from waning supplies of food and water. When that land became a speck in the distance once again and the beast showed no signs of stopping, there wasn't immediate cause for concern. Perhaps the island was barren and unpopulated, and wouldn't have been able to provide what they need to restore both themselves and their vessel. Perhaps the beast knew this, and was saving them once again.

When the second island came and went, anxiety began to creep in like sea fog - slowly at first, and then so overwhelmingly that it blinds you.

prompt five
christmas jumper

THE CHRISTMAS JUMPER
by Hannah Hopkins Jones

I have a Christmas jumper,
It lives under my bed.
As seasons change, it gets in range,
And leaps over my head.

Most people's Christmas jumpers
Can't jump all on their own.
But this one does, and that's because
It's from an elf, on loan.

It's green and red and silver;
All other knitwear pales.
And all year long it's oh-so good,
On threat of New Year's sales.

CHRIS-MAS
by Lucy Hancock

It was Chris' favourite day of the year. Nope, not the big day itself, or even his birthday - both of which are in December. His favourite day, hands down, without question, was National Christmas Jumper Day.

And while he'd heard it too many times to count, he loved when people pointed out (as if he didn't already know!) what a coincidence it was that A) his name was Chris B) he was born in December. Every time, it brought him joy. Like he'd been chosen by God to be the most festive person to walk the earth.

So, when it came to that all important day of the year, Chris opened his jumper-specific wardrobe (with over 255 Christmas jumpers in it, to be precise) and selected his favourite festive jumper of all. One he hadn't yet worn to the office in the seven years he'd worked there. You see, having such a wide selection of Christmas jumpers meant he was never an outfit repeater for these occasions. One couldn't wear the same Christmas jumper two years in a row. That was simply blasphemy.

With a very proud grin on his face (covered by the very white beard he was growing out specifically for December), he walked to the office, which was only a short walk from his flat. Today was going to be a good day. He'd saved this jumper for a very special reason you see.

Exactly 59 days ago, Julie joined Card-mas - you guessed it, the Christmas card manufacturing company. It could be said Chris truly found his dream job the day he joined the place. And exactly 59 days ago, Chris knew Julie was the woman he'd been searching for. He also knew today, National Christmas Jumper Day, was going to be *the* day. The day he would finally pluck up the courage to ask her to accompany him for a drink.

Chris walked into work at precisely 8:52 - just enough time to make his peppermint hot chocolate and log on. Proudly, he unzipped his jacket for the grand reveal before sitting at his desk, his cheeks burning from smiling quite so much.

"C'mon Chris, stand up, let us see!" Dave chuckled, knowing full well just how much Chris, well, loved Christmas.

This was the moment Chris had waited for. Up he stood, just as Julie walked into the office.

He faced Dave, but his eyes were only on Julie. That was, until she spotted his jumper.

"Oh god Chris, *really?*" she said in disgust.

Chris' heart sank.

The woman of his dreams, the moment he was waiting for - ruined. "I can't stand George Michael."

Chris, in his vintage Wham! masterpiece of a jumper, held back his tears. Today wasn't his day after all.

THE CHRISTMAS JUMPER
by Sam JT Butterworth

The icy grey water ran fast and far below. A reluctant snow had just begun and the wind cut through Angus' insubstantial wax jacket, and the polyester Christmas pudding jumper he had on underneath. He'd thought the jacket would give him a vibe of country gent in the city, but it was useless in weather like this, and its deep, earthy smell seemed to hang around him on the bus or the tube, and he worried that it bothered other commuters.

He wasn't on the bus tonight, or the tube. He'd turned left out of his office and walked without thought for 20 minutes. It was then he found himself on Tower Bridge, waiting on the right-hand pavement among clusters of other pedestrians who were wrapped up warmer than him. The bridge was up and a gunmetal grey superyacht was cruising towards the gap. The yacht heightened Angus' feeling of having wasted his 42 years on earth, and this seemed to allow the cold to cut even deeper into him, into the very marrow of his bones.

When the bridge was down again and movement recommenced among the other pedestrians, Angus found himself on the outside of the railings, looking down at the dirty water. His fingers were cold on the metal and he wondered if they'd go numb soon and just cease to work, making his decision for him. He realised he was crying. His knackered brown brogues stuck out over the Thames, the rubber heels shifting a little on the only part of bridge beneath him. The railing was too cold, his fingers couldn't hang on any more, so they let go. Angus closed his eyes.

He opened them. He was still on the bridge. He looked at his hands, both of them in front of him. And then he felt the arms. Five arms wrapped around his torso and two others holding his legs from the other side of the railings. Voices came to him now and he turned. Eyes connected with his, and for right now, this connection was enough.

prompt six
question the heroic approach

CHOCOLATE 3
by Mike Jeavons

Jason loved dogs. He'd grown up with them, and they'd been in his family since he was four years old and his dad brought home a golden retriever called Spud.

There'd been plenty of other dogs since Spud:

Marmalade.

Chocolate (who died after eating chocolate - irony).

Bisto.

Chocolate 2 (that one was run over).

Biscuit.

Jason wasn't sure why all the dogs in his family had been named after food. Maybe it was something to do with the fact his family all loved food (they received a Christmas card from the local takeaway every year) as much as they seemed to love dogs.

Which was why Jason didn't hesitate in saving the dog from the oncoming car.

He did it!

He was a hero!

The chocolate lab (which wasn't called Chocolate - why?!) ran out of the road and into the park without a scratch on him.

Trouble was, in saving the dog Jason had killed an eighty-three-year-old woman called Theresa Baker - which was, funnily enough, another food-related name belonging to somebody/something that had died.

Jason felt great because he watched as the chocolate lab was put on his leash and led - presumably - home by its owner. However, he also felt knots form in his stomach on account of the pensioner lodged beneath his bumper.

But she'd had a good innings, right? That's something that people said when somebody old dies. Even if the cause of death was a little questionable.

Or, as Jason soon discovered after he was placed in handcuffs and into the back of a police car, *very* questionable. Then, as he stood in the dock and was ordered by the judge to spend seven years in prison, very *very* questionable.

But at least a Facebook group was set up by Gemma, twenty-nine from Southampton, declaring Jason a hero because it was rumoured Theresa Baker once wore a jacket with a swastika patch sewn on the elbow. The group had 97 likes - nice!

However, the group called *Jason Rivers should rot in hell* had a few more likes.

305,643 to be exact.

HERO
by Lucy Hancock

EXT. FAMILY GARDEN

Enter from stage left, two young brothers aged
five and seven are in their back garden.

TOMMY: WHO'S YOUR FAVOURITE, GEORGE? I LOVE THOR.
HE'S SO... *BIG*.

George, Tommy's older brother, is walking ahead
of him across the grass. He approaches a large
oak tree at the bottom of the garden.

TOMMY: GEORGE?

GEORGE (sighing): TOMMY, PLEASE BE QUIET. I'M
PLANNING.

TOMMY: WHAT DO YOU MEAN?

George circles the tree, facing away from his
brother. He lifts his leg up the tree trunk and
pulls himself up with his right arm.

TOMMY: GEORGE! WHAT ARE YOU DOING? MUMMY TOLD US WE CAN'T CLIMB THE -

GEORGE: SHUSH, TOMMY, THEY'LL HEAR US!

Tommy looks behind them, looks back at his brother, then looks across the garden. Sounds of a dog barking and a woman talking from the house can be heard.

GEORGE: PROBABLY IRON MAN. BUT I DON'T NEED A SUIT TO FLY, TOMMY.

George is now three feet above the ground and is balancing on a tree branch. Tommy is pacing back and forth, circling the tree trunk, a fearful look across his face.

TOMMY: GEORGE, BE CAREFUL!

The younger brother is scared, he bites his fingernails and his voice is becoming more high-pitched.

GEORGE: I'LL SHOW YOU, HANG ON I -

TOMMY: GEORGE, YOU NEED TO GET DOWN NOW!

GEORGE: TOMMY, BE QUIET, MUMMY WILL HEAR US

George is struggling to find his balance, the branch of the tree is shaking.

GEORGE: LOOK TOMMY, I CAN FLY!

Tommy screams.

Blackout.

Fifteen-Minute Fiction: a flash fiction anthology

QUESTION: THE HEROIC APPROACH?
by Sam JT Butterworth

So the question came up in my mind, bright and urgent, and demanding an answer. Dare I go for the heroic approach?

One more minute, I told myself. One more minute, then I'll do it. Was there even a heroic approach? I thought there might be, if I tackled it right.

I remembered her face, if vaguely, from earlier on in the Irish bar. She was beautiful, in an elfin, slightly too-much-makeup, Cindy Lauper kind of way. It was pretty late then.

Now it was later and I was in trouble. I needed to summon up some courage. I couldn't crouch behind this locked door all night. Did I think it would just go away if I did nothing? No, I definitely didn't think that. That would be optimistic. Doing something hadn't helped, had it?

Could this be saved? Did I even like her? Did I like her enough?

I flicked back the chrome lock of the chipped bathroom door and walked upright into the dimly lit living room, which smelled of incense and vodka. I looked at the girl, walked straight past her and ran out into the street and homeward, leaving her to discover the unflushable consequences of 8 pints of Guinness and a large doner kebab.

prompt seven

a frog runs into the house

SPLAT
by Lucy Hancock

Leapt further than planned.
Spindly legs miss the window…
A green frog, now red.

AN IMPORTANT NEWS UPDATE
by Mike Jeavons

BREAKING NEWS

London, February 2023: East London was the scene of a tragedy last night, when a woman was found dead by a pizza delivery man. David, 23 from Dominos, said 'I feel a bit peaky, to be honest. I turned up on time with her double pepperoni surprise, when I saw her lying there, covered in pond water.'

The victim, an unidentified woman thought to be in her 50s and living close to the local tow path, was discovered expired on her doorstep. The Dominos driver called for an ambulance, but the victim was pronounced dead at the scene.

Police were also in attendance, and have arrested a small, green frog, 1, who presumably resides in the nearby canal.

In a statement, Police Constable Smith said, 'Ordinarily we wouldn't arrest amphibians for murder, however, the frog was known by the victim.'

It's thought that the pizza-loving victim's son once kept the suspect as a pet, and lived in a vivarium in his bedroom. However, the victim had a well-publicised fear of frogs, having published her memoir, *I Fucking Hate Frogs*. Allegedly, the victim released the suspect into the canal, where she thought he would be eaten by a heron. However, it's believed that the frog made his way back to the victims home, and stabbed her with a kitchen knife, which was still in his hands when police arrived.

More on this story as it develops.

CATCHING FLIES
by Hannah Hopkins Jones

The door slammed, and Frances heard the *pat pat pat* of her husband's webbed toes running through to the kitchen.

'Freddie?' When her call was met by silence she eased herself away from her desk and went to investigate.

In the kitchen, her husband of several years, Fredward D. Frog, seemed to be intent on emptying the contents of every cupboard onto the floor.

'You were right, Franny,' he panted, a thin sheen of sweat lying atop the usual mucus membrane on his speckled green brow, 'you were right about everything.'

Normally this phrase would have been music to Frances' ears no matter the context, but her husband's distress was so unnerving (and ridiculous) that she decided to swallow back her desire to gloat. She watched Fredward reach into a high cupboard, grab a jar of mustard and then quickly discard it onto the linoleum where it (mercifully) bounced and rolled away.

'Oh really?' Frances arranged her expression into suitable nonchalance. 'What about?'

'I should have never listened to that pushy salesman,' Fredward muttered, more to himself than to his wife, his hands finally descending on the condiment he'd been searching for. He raised the jar of golden honey over his head, triumphant, and then turned to head for the door.

'I knew the advertisement was simply too good to be true. Well, I didn't know *then*, but I know *now*! I'll show him. How many years have I been in this business? How long have I been putting food on this table? How could I possibly fall for that conman's scheme!'

Still in a frenzy, Fredward went to hurry past Frances, doubling back only to pop a quick kiss to her cheek before breaking into a run once more. Frances sighed, surveying the state of the kitchen. She caught the end of her husband's ranting and raving before the front door swung shut behind him.

'Vinegar! *Vinegar*? What was I *thinking*!'

THE FROG
by Sam JT Butterworth

The frog ran into the house. But of course it didn't because frogs don't run. It hopped - although they don't even hop really, do they? Not on one leg anyway - that'd be weird. Let's start again - the frog jumped into the house. My house to be specific. Why? You'd have to ask the frog. I should ask the frog? Well, alright, but I don't know what you're expecting really.

So Frog, erm… This is stupid... OK, OK. So Frog, can you please explain in your *finest* English why you, er, made your way into my house?

Thought you'd never ask, dear boy!

Oh, you're talking.

Be hard to explain otherwise wouldn't it, me old fruit? Were you expecting charades? Pictionary? Not so good at those with the old webbed digits.

OK, go on then.

Don't mind if I do. I popped out of the pond for a run around your pleasant little garden...

A run?

Yes, a run. Problem with that, old love?

Forget it, go on.

So I hopped out of the old pond and was stretching the old cuisses de grenouilles...

What?

Frog's legs, old boy. May I please continue?

Aprés vous.

In fact they come into it, rather. So I was bounding around in nature, enjoying the sun on my back and the breeze in my snout, when next door's new tom cat got a whiff of me and pelted over the fence and began to give chase. Beastly blighter.

OK, that makes sense.

So in I popped, sure a lovey like you wouldn't mind an amphibian friend hopping in to say hello.

Hopping? Like on one leg?

Bit of a bloody pedant aren't you, darling?

Well, that may be. But that cat that was chasing you - that's not next door's new cat, it's mine. And there's the cat flap, right behind you. And I hear the sound of approaching paws.

prompt eight
write one sentence, carry it on 2

THE YELLOW SOFA

by Sam JT Butterworth, Lucy Hancock, Mike Jeavons and Hannah
Hopkins Jones, each taking turns to write one sentence

The yellow sofa needed repairs. **It was currently being supported
by three legs, only two of which matched, and a stack of
unloved books.** *Some might say, it was a magical sofa…* Especially after
dark. Rumour has it, on one day a year, sitting on the sofa allowed
you to travel back in time.

**The sofa had changed hands several times in its life, and
currently resided in the back of a boardgame cafe.** *Hidden beneath
a dusty, crumb-covered sheet, little did the local board game nerds know about its
spooktacular abilities.* Until one foggy evening when Clive, Sarah and
Waltraud took their hot chocolates to the back of the cafe and sat
on the yellow couch.

"Christ, this is one uncomfortable sofa," Sarah huffed.

**Clive had been just about to reply, when abruptly the music in
the cafe changed - Doja Cat was silenced, and replaced by a
brassy melody.**

"What hath just entered my chambers?" bellowed the fat old man, sat on the edge of his four-poster bed. The three board-gamers looked around and realised that the old yellow sofa was now positioned in a large, high-ceilinged bedroom decorated as if it was the 17th century.

Waltraud removed his outrageously over-sized glasses from his face and wiped them with the cuff of his jumper, as if doing so would add some clarity to the bizarre situation. **Meanwhile, the man on the bed was shrugging his way into an extravagantly embroidered velvet dressing gown.**

"Who's this clown?" asked Clive, "Some sort of Henry the Eighth cosplayer or something?"

'Silence fool,' said the big man, 'I am clearly Henry the fucking 7th!'

Sarah was yet to say anything - too distracted by the grumpy, unbrushed cat that had just walked through the door.

"You know," Waltraud - a cat person through and through - immediately got up to stroke the cat, "as VR goes, this isn't half bad considering what we paid."

"STOP THAT AT ONCE," screamed Henry the fucking 7th, "GET YOUR HANDS OFF MY LUNCH."

Just then the three time travellers (?) realised that the books holding up the yellow sofa hadn't travelled (?) with them and the thing collapsed, sending them rolling to Henry's gout-riddled feet.

Clive gagged. "When was the last time you bathed?"

Sarah was about to express a similar sentiment when she noticed, to her dismay, that the sofa was beginning to disintegrate into thin air.

Waltraud panicked and scrambled back to the yellow, moth-eaten sofa, but Clive struggled to get his footing as Henry's massive sausage-fingered hand grabbed hold of his shoulder.

'I don't fucking think so!' he bellowed. 'I've been trying to get this sofa back for centuries!'

prompt nine
refusing to sleep

NIGHT RIDE
by Sam JT Butterworth

Heavy eyelids part

Dad's car keys wait on their hook

Velvet blackness calls

THE MAN IN THE SHADOWS
by Mike Jeavons

'Go to sleep.'

'No.'

'Daniel, go to sleep.'

'NO.'

'For f—yes. Please.'

'I can't, Mumma.'

'Why?'

'They'll get me.'

'Who will get you?'

'The man in the shadows.'

'What man? What shadows? You could land aircraft using your nightlight.'

'He turns it off.'

'Who does?'

'The man in the shadows.'

'There's nobody here, darling. Look. Nobody by the wardrobe, nobody by the door, nobody under the bed. See.'

'I saw him.'

'When?'

'Last night and the night before and the night before that.'

'Was it Daddy?'

'No.'

'Was it Grandad?'

'No.'

'Then who was it?'

'I don't know.'

'You were just dreaming, sweetheart. Goodni—'

'NO MUMMY PLEASE.'

'Daniel, for goodness' sake.'

'He'll hurt me.'

'Dreams can be scary, but they don't hurt us.'

'They do.'

'No, they don't.'

'The man in the shadows does.'

'Hun. No.'

'He does I promise, he hurt me last night.'

'What did he do?'

'He bit me.'

'It was all in your dream, sweetie.'

'It wasn't, look.'

'...'

'See I told you, Mummy.'

'Did your brother do that to you?'

'No.'

'Did he tell you to lie to me?'

No.'

'Did somebody at school?'

'No, it was the man in the shadows.'

'Daniel. Please.'

'I swear to you, Mummy.'

'Daniel, I promise. You believe Mummy when she makes a promise, don't you? That's right, so please believe me when I tell you that there's no man in the shadows.'

'There is.'

'It's probably just your brother being a little—being naughty.'

'No, it's not because the man in the shadows is taller than him. He's even taller than Daddy.'

'Really, now?'

'Yes, and he said next time he sees me he's going to hurt me even worserer than last time.'

'He isn't. There is no man. There are no shadows. There's just… your dreams.'

'Then Mummy…'

'Yes?'

'Who's that standing behind you?'

NETFLIX AND CHILL
by Lucy Hancock

My mother is a hypochondriac. Any problem, whether it's a headache or a pimple - she'll turn to Google. Once, she *diagnosed* me with stomach cancer because I hadn't been to the loo for a couple of days. Turns out avoiding vegetables isn't too great for your digestive system. *Who knew?*

Anyway.

She's at it again. She noticed the glow of my lamp under the door frame when she got up for the bathroom at four A.M. The next morning, as I'm making my way through my third cup of coffee before 8:30, she turns to me as I'm mid-mouthful of cornflakes.

'Jim, I think you have insomnia. I'm extremely worried about you. In fact, I think you need to see Daniel.'

I choke and the cornflakes very nearly make it out of my mouth and onto the dining table. Daniel is our GP. My Mother calls him by his first name because, as you may have gathered, she spends a lot of time at the doctor. I'm convinced she's worried about her health or *really* fancies Dr. Graham (Daniel). Probably the latter.

'What?' I say in disbelief, not quite catching her gaze that stares at me intently.

'I've noticed you're awake, *every* single night. Your Father got up twice for the toilet last night and he noticed it too.'

I sigh. 'I've just been struggling to sleep, Mum. I'm absolutely fine. Honestly.'

'Jim,' she interrupts.

'Mum,' I stand and put the breakfast bowl into the sink. 'It's just nice to have the free time, you know? At uni, I'm always *so* exhausted from all the essays and the books and the -'

She shakes her head. 'I know dear, I know you work hard.'

I'm lying. My Dad is smirking to himself while reading the paper, he knows it too.

The reality? I'm binge-watching Doctor Who for the fifth time this summer. I can't help myself.

prompt ten
a memorable car ride

SPIDER, MAN
by Mike Jeavons

There was a spider in my car. I hate spiders quite a lot. That's why I set my car on fire.

I didn't do it on purpose. Well, *did* mean to start the fire, but I only intended to burn the spider - not the entire car.

In my defence, it was a massive fucking spider. Think of the biggest spider you've ever seen, then double – no – triple it. It was like *Cousin It* was walking over my steering wheel. In fact, I'm lucky I only destroyed my own car, because when I spotted the beast I yanked the steering wheel so hard I crossed three lanes of traffic.

It's no great loss really - other than the great monetary loss this whole farce will undoubtedly cost me, that is. It was an old car; so old there were no seatbelts in the backseat and there was a tape deck above the cigarette lighter.

It was the cigarette lighter I used to start the fire. Useful, really.

I think I got the spider before the car itself became lost to the flames. The trouble was, I dropped the bloody lighter under the seat, and it rolled into the back footwell. That would ordinarily be fine, but there was a (not quite) empty petrol can also in the back which I'd used to top up the fuel tank when I ran the thing dry the week before.

The explosion was quite spectacular. I managed to snap a photo on my phone. I wonder if I'll be able to sell it to the papers and make some money back to buy a new car.

Probably not. I bet someone's already uploaded their dashcam footage of my entire ordeal to Tik Tok.

THE TOYOTA AND THE SMILE
by Sam JT Butterworth

Flames licked from the open passenger door of the old, rust-flecked Toyota. She watched it burn until the tyres popped with shocking, plosive thumps. The windows cracked and eventually broke and more flames climbed out of the car and reached for the indigo sky, getting there only as smoke, sickly and acrid and wrong-smelling.

Why had she come back? Why couldn't she have carried on walking - even hitched a ride to town - made her escape? She knew the answer. Because it wouldn't feel like an escape unless she watched it burn down to twisted aluminium and charred seat springs. And what else?

The smoke caught in her throat but she didn't resist it. The heat burned her bruised, tear-stained face but she didn't step back. Instead she stood rigid in the melting snow, looking through the open door to the driver's seat, at the coiled shape draped over the steering wheel. The shape that hadn't noticed her gently unfasten his seatbelt, and hadn't expected her to grab the wheel and steer them straight into that snow-decked pine tree. She watched the shape as flames danced around it and engulfed it and consumed it. And she smiled.

SETTING FIRE TO THE CAR
by Lucy Hancock

Since being a child, I always knew my Mother was different. Her answer to what she did for work changed weekly. Aged five, this was just a game we used to play. One week, she was a zookeeper. Over dinner, she'd tell me about all the animals she'd cared for. The next week, she was a famous novelist touring the country on a book tour. Until the age of ten, I never really thought much of it. My Mum was the coolest Mum of them all because she changed who she was whenever she liked.

Aged fifteen, I first discovered the clue that got the ball rolling. In our basement, on a Thursday evening. My Mum was away on business, and at this point I didn't ask any questions as to the job she now did.

That's when I found the weapons, the wigs and the several passports. Each passport was her face, but with a different hair colour and a name I couldn't pronounce.

And that was why I had to set fire to her most prized possession. The Land Rover Discovery sitting on our driveway.

WAVE ME DOWN
by Hannah Hopkins Jones

It's funny, because now that the smoke is rising I feel as if everyone who sees this will perceive tonight the same way that I am. That's useful, because I don't think I could do it justice in words. There's been this deep gauze over everything since I woke up back there, and now that you mention it, it really does remind me of smoke. I know that this smog should hit me in the back of the throat, and grasp the place where my senses collide and hang there, cloying, but I really can't get a feeling for it. It's far away even though I'm standing right next to it. I inhale but it doesn't touch my lungs.

I've never seen a car flip before, and a little part of me reckons my brother would have said it was cool and then apologised, but not meant it. Psychopath. I don't think you needed to swerve the way that you did when I stepped out to greet you because, if I'm being honest, I don't feel very solid right now. When that thing - person, club, thug, end, stop, no - hit me in the back of the head, it's like it knocked all of the solid out of me, used up my solid quota, and being dense and heavy isn't something I'm allowed to do anymore. Must have been a few hours ago now. Fire's getting high. Wish I could feel it.

Anyway, the explosion was really loud - even *I* can tell it was loud and I'm not sure my ears are working anymore - so someone will come out and find you soon. Maybe in finding you they'll find me. Maybe if I stick around I'll see you get right up out of the car like I got up out of the ditch, and we can pal around a bit, shoot the crap. I know I was at home no more than half a day ago, but I felt like I'd been on my own for a hundred years before I saw your car. I know that doesn't make sense, but maybe you'll understand.

There are headlights coming. I hope they can see us. I think I'll go wave them down, just to be safe.

ABOUT THE AUTHORS

Sam JT Butterworth is a managing editor, fiction writer, copywriter and former journalist, with a steadily increasing line of dependents, and a rapidly decreasing amount of free time.

Lucy Hancock is a poet, fiction writer, copywriter and all-round creative human. You'll usually find her stroking a cat and crying over Taylor Swift. She's yet to grow out of writing dramatic, emo poetry.

Mike Jeavons is an author, screenwriter, copywriter and editor, who somehow also finds time to visit theme parks, watch movies, and be a best-selling pseudonymous satirist.

Hannah Hopkins Jones is a creative, fiction writer, and copywriter, who aspires to be a 'jack of all trades', and an eventual master of at least one. She has written for stage and screen, competes both nationally and internationally with her roller derby team, and will avoid having to cook at all costs

Special thanks to **Davey Rees** for his expertise in helping design the cover.

Printed in Great Britain
by Amazon

23614771R00056